JUL'1 5

W9-AER-084

For D.M.B. —D. C.

For my longtime neighbor, Jean —R. L.

VIKING

Published by the Penguin Group

Penguin Group (USA) LLC

375 Hudson Street

New York, New York 10014

USA ✦ Canada ✦ UK ✦ Ireland ✦ Australia ✦ New Zealand ✦ India ✦ South Africa ✦ China

penguin.com

A Penguin Random House Company

First published in the United States of America by Viking, an imprint of Penguin Young Readers Group, 2015

Text copyright © 2015 by Doreen Cronin

Illustrations copyright © 2015 by Renata Liwska

Penguin supports copyright. Copyright fuels creativity, encourages diverse voices, promotes free speech, and creates a vibrant culture.

Thank you for buying an authorized edition of this book and for complying with copyright laws by not reproducing, scanning, or distributing

any part of it in any form without permission. You are supporting writers and allowing Penguin to continue to publish books for every reader.

LIBRARY OF CONGRESS CATALOGING-IN-PUBLICATION DATA IS AVAILABLE

ISBN: 978-0-670-78577-3

Manufactured in China

1   3   5   7   9   10   8   6   4   2

Book design by Nancy Brennan   Set in Ionic MT

Boom Snot Twitty
this way
that way

Doreen Cronin ✳ *illustrated by* Renata Liwska

Viking

An Imprint of Penguin Group (USA)

Boom, Snot, and Twitty
hit the trail early
to find the perfect spot
to spend the day.

"The perfect spot," said Boom,
"is this way."

"The perfect spot," said Twitty,
"is that way."

"Hmmm," said Snot.

"I have everything we need
for the beach!" said Boom.

"I have everything we need
for the mountains!" cried Twitty.

"I have snacks," said Snot.

"What do you want to do at the beach?"
asked Snot.

"Jump and splash," said Boom.

"Of course," said Snot.

"What do you want to do in the mountains?"
asked Snot.

"Hike and look," said Twitty.

"Naturally," said Snot.

Boom put on his flippers and his goggles.

"I want to jump and splash!" said Boom.

"I want to hike and look," said Twitty.
She put on her boots and picked up
her binoculars.

Boom blew up his tube.

"I'm hungry."

Twitty unrolled her hammock.
"I'm tired."

"May I have some of your snack, Snot?"
asked Boom.

Snot did not answer.

"Snot?" said Boom.

He looked under his tube

and inside his flippers.

No Snot.

"Snot?" said Twitty.

She looked under her boots

and through her binoculars.

No Snot.

On the ground
they found
a trail of blueberries.

"This way!" cried Twitty.
Twitty followed the trail carefully,
hiking quickly through the hills.

"That way!" said Boom.

Boom followed the trail with his nose,

jumping and splashing
along the edge of a stream.

"I think this is the perfect spot,"
declared Snot.

"Of course!" said Boom.

"Naturally!" said Twitty.

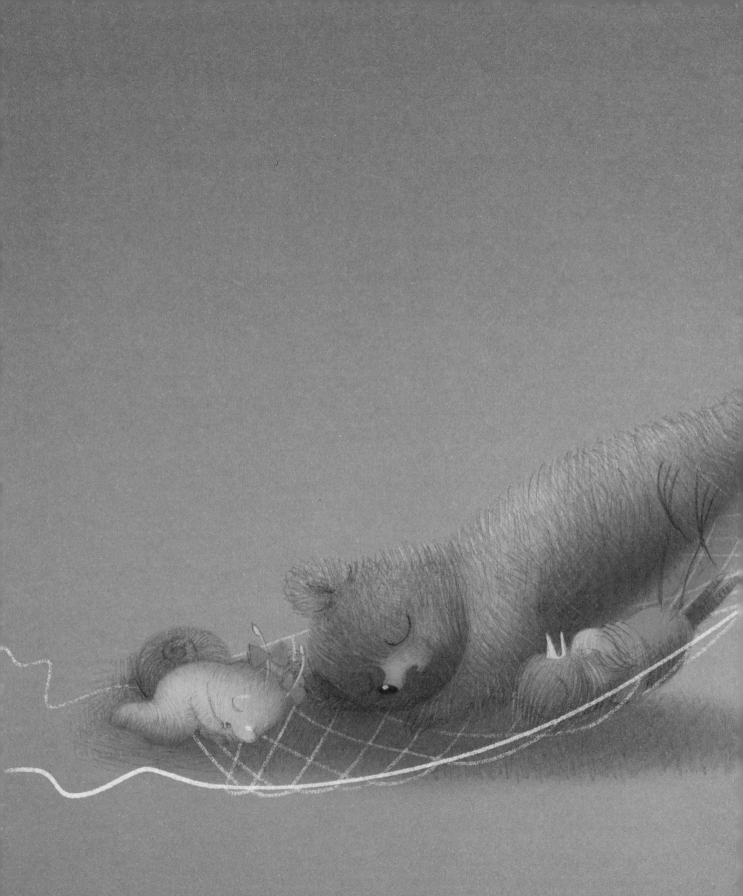